MISSING MOLLY

Lisa Jahn-Clough

HOUGHTON MIFFLIN COMPANY BOSTON 2000

Walter Lorraine Books

For:
Anne, Hilary, James, Jeff, Mary, Matt,
Pam, Robb, Thomas, Tom, and Walter

Walter Lorraine (wл) Books

Copyright © 2000 by Lisa Jahn-Clough

Library of Congress Cataloging-in-Publication Data

Jahn-Clough, Lisa.
    Missing Molly / by Lisa Jahn-Clough.
        p.   cm.
    Summary: When Simon goes to visit his next-door neighbor Molly, he
cannot find her anywhere until a strange girl in a big hat, dark
glasses, and a feather boa appears at the door.
    ISBN 0-618-00980-9
    [1. Hide-and-seek Fiction.   2. Neighbors Fiction.   3. Best friends
Fiction.   4. Friendship Fiction.]   I. Title.
PZ7.J153536SI   2000
[E] — dc21   99-20825
    R   CIP
    PHR 10 9 8 7 6 5 4 3 2 1

Simon and Molly live next
door to each other.
They play together every day.
Their favorite game is
hide-and-seek.

Whenever Simon is it,
Molly hides under the sink.
"You're too easy to find,"
he said one day. "This is no fun."
"Hmmm," Molly said.

The next time Simon looked under
the sink Molly was not there.
Simon looked under the bed.
"Still too easy!" he said.
"Hmmm," Molly said.

The next day when Simon knocked
on Molly's door there was no answer.
"Hello!" he said.
No answer.
"Anybody home?" he said.
No answer.
"I'm here to play!" he shouted.

"Molly must be hiding already,"
Simon thought.
He looked under the sink.
No Molly.

Simon looked under the bed. No Molly.

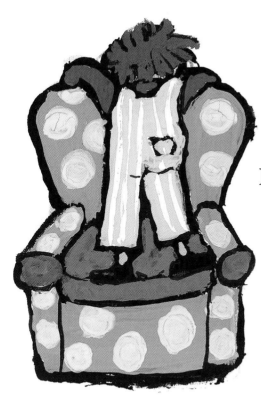

He looked behind the chair

and in the broom closet.

He looked in the laundry hamper and in the toy box.

Finally he looked in the refrigerator, where he helped himself to some grapes. But Molly was nowhere to be found.

"Where could she be?" Simon wondered.

Suddenly there was a noise from the kitchen.
Simon ran to surprise Molly,
but it was only the cat.
"Molly is missing!" Simon shouted.
"Meow!" the cat said.

Just then there was a knock on the door.
A strange girl stood on the steps.
"Hello. I'm looking for Molly,"
she said in a low voice.

"Me too! I came over to play
and I can't find her anywhere," said Simon.
"That's odd. Did you look
under the sink?" the girl asked.
"I looked everywhere," Simon said.
"Hmmm," the girl said. "Maybe she's outside."

The girl looked behind the bushes.
"No Molly here," she said.

She looked up the maple tree.
"No Molly here," she said.

She looked in
the flowerpot
and under
the doormat.

Finally she checked her bag.
"No Molly anywhere," she said.

"What will I do?" Simon asked.
"Maybe you could play with
me," the strange girl said.
"I can't now," Simon said.
"Why not?" the girl asked.
"Because I have to find Molly. She
is my very best friend," Simon said.

The girl took off her dark sunglasses.

"Molly!" Simon shouted.

"I was just hiding on you," Molly said.

"This was the best hiding idea ever,"
said Simon. "I thought you were gone for good."

"I'd never do that," Molly said.

"Why not?" Simon asked.

"Because you're my very best friend, too!"

And the very best friends went off to play.